Disney

Hundred-Acre Adv

Bad Mood

D0537749

Ladybird

When Rabbit entered his garden one morning, he knew it was the sort of day when his friends would say, 'Rabbit is in a bad mood!'

His carrots had shrunk, the lettuce had wilted, and the turnips had simply forgotten to grow. He knelt down to pull a radish.

'Oh, what a disaster!' he cried as he took a bite. 'It's too hot and spicy!'

He pulled out another one and another one, but they were as hot as the first.

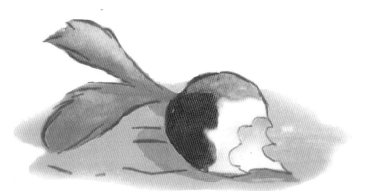

Rabbit turned to his shrunken carrots. Without a word, he pulled them out and threw them as far away as he could.

He looked at his ruined garden, and his bad mood got worse.

'Disaster of disasters!' he said as he jumped up and down.

That's when Rabbit saw Tigger bouncing towards him.

'I'm impressed, Bunny Boy!' Tigger said as Rabbit continued to jump in anger. 'I didn't know you could bounce so well! Will you come and bounce with me?'

'Tigger, I am not in the mood to be merry,' said Rabbit, crossly.

'Really? Well, I'd better go then!' shouted Tigger as he bounced away.

'There! Now I'm on my own,' groaned Rabbit. 'Alone with these wilted lettuce leaves that are only good to be stepped on!' he concluded.

There was not much left of
Rabbit's garden when Piglet arrived.
He had thought that Rabbit would be
happy to see him, but seeing Rabbit's
cross face he wasn't so sure.

'Good morning, Rabbit,' Piglet
whispered.

'What do you want?'
mumbled Rabbit. 'Can't you
see I'm in a bad mood?'

'Well, yes Rabbit, I can
see that! Oh dear, look at your
garden. All the vegtables have
been pulled out!' said Piglet.

'I think you'd better go, Piglet,' said Rabbit. 'My bad mood is growing bigger.'

Piglet looked in fright above Rabbit's head. Since he could see nothing there, he thought he must be too small to see such a big, bad mood.

Piglet started to tremble. If Rabbit's bad mood came too close, it might gobble him up!

'G–goodbye, Rabbit!' Piglet stuttered.

Piglet ran straight to Pooh's house to tell him what was going on.

'I see,' said Pooh as he thought hard. 'Rabbit doesn't like being in a bad mood.'

Pooh understood so well.

'You say the bad mood is above Rabbit's head, but you can't see it?' asked Pooh, as he thought even harder.

'Yes,' confirmed Piglet.

'Dear me,' said Pooh.
'I think the bad mood is
some sort of cloud which
stops Rabbit from being
in a good mood.'
'Maybe it's like a storm inside
his head,' suggested Piglet.
'It looked like there was
lightning in Rabbit's eyes.'

The friends went to Owl's house to ask him what he thought.

'If Rabbit is in a bad mood, and he doesn't like being in a bad mood,' Owl reasoned wisely, 'then the bad mood must be removed from him.'

'With water, to put out the lightning in his eyes?' asked Piglet.

'By blowing away the cloud above his head?' suggested Pooh.

'I think we should try to understand why Rabbit is in a bad mood,' Owl said. 'Then Rabbit's bad mood will go away by itself.'

The three friends headed off to Rabbit's house. Tigger bounced by and joined them.

They found Rabbit in the same spot, leaning on his shovel with an angry face.

'So, I hear you're in a bad mood,' said Owl.

'Can't you see?' grumbled Rabbit.

'We would like to know why you are in a bad mood,' Owl continued.

Rabbit waved his arm at his ruined garden.

'Shrunken carrots, yellow lettuce, hot radishes and not even the smallest little turnip!' he said.

'Could it be that you might have forgotten to water your plants?' Owl reasoned.

Rabbit clutched his shovel. Piglet was sure he saw streaks of lightning in his eyes.

'Are you suggesting that I did not do my job properly!' cried Rabbit, angrily.

Spreading his wings, Owl turned to his friends. 'This is what I call being in a bad mood,' he said.

'Yes, I am in a bad mood!' cried Rabbit, losing his temper. 'I won't have enough food for winter, and now you're calling me a bad gardener!'

'Of course we know that you haven't made a mistake,' protested Owl. 'You are an excellent gardener!'

'Could it be worms eating Rabbit's seeds?' suggested Piglet.

'Impossible. Gopher ate all the worms last spring,' grumbled Rabbit as Gopher poked his little face out of a hole.

'What if the turnip seeds were still in your cellar and not in the ground at all?' suggested Tigger.

'Hmmm,' muttered Rabbit. Rabbit tried to remember. Now he thought about it, he wasn't so sure that he'd actually planted the seeds at all!

'Maybe it was the bad weather,' added Pooh. 'It rained so much this year. Do you remember we had to cancel a picnic?'

'Oh yes!' recalled Piglet. 'There were so many puddles!'

'And I missed the most beautiful bounce when I got stuck in the mud!' cried Tigger.

'No plants could grow in such conditions,' confirmed Owl.

'This must be what happened!' exclaimed Rabbit with a smile forming from ear to ear.

'We will help you plant your garden all over again!' declared Pooh.

'Your vegetables will still have plenty of time to grow before winter!'

'If someone asked my opinion about all of this, but I bet no one will,' grumbled Eeyore, 'I would say that a bad mood is like bad weather. It comes and goes, just as the sky can be blue or grey.'

'Aren't Eeyores always grey?' Rabbit asked.

Eeyore nodded, and everyone laughed as they helped a happy Rabbit tend to his garden.